Lizzie I. Beller

The Star of Light

Lizzie I. Beller

The Star of Light

ISBN/EAN: 9783337409012

Printed in Europe, USA, Canada, Australia, Japan

Cover: Foto ©Andreas Hilbeck / pixelio.de

More available books at **www.hansebooks.com**

THE

STAR

OF ...

LIGHT

To the Masonic Fraternity—

Who have ever been as the "Shadow of a Great Rock in a Weary Land," and to those who have "Seen His Star in the East," this volume is courteously and respectfully dedicated.

LIZZIE I. BELLER.

The Blue Veil.

When formless was the earth and void,
  Before the world awoke,
While darkness moved upon the deep,
  E'er yet Jehovah spoke ;
In that vast realm of chaos,
  All nature's forces grand,
Lay wrapped in sleep and silence deep
  Awaiting God's command.
'Tis told in the Sacred Story
  That over that Gulf of Night
He sent a ray of His Glory—
  He said, "Let there be Light."
His spirit moved in its mighty power
  Over the misty deep,

And all the waters from that hour
  Into their cradle creep,
And there the Earth forever rocks
  The Ocean waves to sleep.
And when He breathed upon that world
  Where lay the darksome night,
A luminous haze of ether blue

Was the first born ray of light.
It circling spread, like a fleecy cloud,
  And covered the darkness o'er,
The very first Veil of azure pale'
  That earth and Heaven wore.
It rose, a mist, of amethyst,
  In the sky its station was given,
To curtain the world with its light unfurled,
  And to hide the earth from Heaven.
Never a shade does its azure fade,
  A type of eternal truth ;
It covers us o'er with the blue that it wore
  When time was in its youth.
Watchers abide on the other side,
  But when our loved ones die,
The Veil opens wide to the purified
  That their souls may pass on high.
None but the immortal have crossed its portal
  Save three, where death was denied,
But its beauties reveal the Omnipotent seal
  To mortals who here abide.
Night's fingers unroll the Heavenly scroll,
  The letters are stars of light ;
It is God's own history, written in mystery,
  And language infinite.

        *   *

Joyous sounds the harp and cymbal,
  Victory is in the song ;
Home returning from the battle,
  Jepthah, victor, leads the throng.

Over Gilead. and Manassah,
　And the Ammonitish race,
Waves on high the conquerors' banner,
　Fairly won its honored place.

Won, the meed of his ambition—
　" Jepthah, Judge of Israel " now—
Flushed with pride to see his subjects
　Humble and submissive bow.

Illegitimate and outcast,
　Stainless, honored now, and free ;
Oh ! how roseate glowed the future,
　Only eyes of hope can see.

But memory wakes within him,
　With Mizpah in his view,
His rash vow to Jehovah
　Of fearful import grew.

Adah and her maidens,
　A happy, joyous throng,
Hasten forth to meet him,
　With timbrel, dance and song.

Of what value now his honors,
　Bought at such abhorrent price ?
Could the twenty conquered cities
　Pay for Adah's sacrifice ?

All-consuming is ambition,
　Reaching to its utmost goal ;
When all else is burned to ashes
　It will feed upon the soul.

In this life and in the future,
    Singing its victorious song—
"Know that I shall live forever,
    I to Lucifer belong."

*   *   *   *   *   *

The Rabbis question Adah's fate,
    And cite that all the law
Would bar a human sacrifice,
    Its forfeiture withdraw.
Since none could of that life dispose,
    Which he could not restore,
The flames were those of Moloch,
    Accursed for evermore.
And naught of such a sacrifice,
    If human life was given,
Would be accepted in his sight
    Or reach the God of Heaven.

*   *   *   *   *

There is a story, or legend,
    Which thus defines their fate.
'Tis that in the lowest Paradise
    Jepthah and Adah wait.

Where ever and ever recurs the scene
    Which Adah's fidelity knew ;
She knows no wrong, but Jepthah's sin
    Is ever before his view.

He dare not tell her that fatal hour
　　In the past forever is o'er,
For there, by decree of Omnipotent power,
　　It will live till time is no more.

And there in sorrow his spirit
　　In remorse o'er the past shall brood,
Because of the fatal vow he made
　　And of passion unsubdued.

And ever this truth he repeats,
　　As "Alas, my daughter," he cries
" The voices of wrong to time belong,
　　But eternity always replies."

Adah's memory, lingering on that vow,
　　Unfulfilled to her its import clings,
Ever thus with Jepthah pleads,
　　As of that sacrifice she sings :

" Father, is it not the hour
　　For the promised sacrifice ?
I am ready, then hereafter
　　Comes the joy of Paradise.

" Father, on the mountain's summit,
　　Where it meets the crystal light,
Spirits from the upper Heaven
　　Often pause upon their flight.

" They have told me on the earth-land
　　Many are the changes wrought ;
Israel as a nation vanished,
　　And their greatness come to naught.

" That the Christ became an earth-born,
　　And His teaching to mankind
Shows them where the law of Moses
　　And the law of love combined,

"Forms a brotherhood eternal,
　　Man to man as brothers bind,
In this law of love the living
　　Truth and life eternal find.

"And they say a vow now given
　　For ambition's strange device,
Would not reach the Great Jehovah,
　　Nor would he demand its price.

" Tell they, too, that truth and honor
　　By no sacrifice are bought ;
But instead by earthly barter
　　They are often sold for naught

" Some of this I understood not,
　　And I said that to be true
To the teachings of Jehovah
　　Was the only law I knew.

" Strangely then they gazed upon us,
　　And my maidens timid grew,
While the spirits wondering, whispered,
　　' Is that earthly story true ?'

"Art thou, then, that 'Jepthah's daughter,'
　　Who to prove a sacrifice,
Taught the world that living lesson,
　　Honor is without a price ?

"Saying, then, that in the earth-world,
  Where abides the human race,
Jepthah's daughter and her story
  Have an high, an honored place.

"That the lesson I had taught them
  Was repeated night by night,
Someone, somewhere, ever leading
  Out of darkness into light.

" Brightest of the Orient jewels
  Shining in the Eastern Star,
Light and knowledge, and the beauty
  Of a soul no sin could mar.

' Wondrous stories, too, they told me
  Of another, brighter sphere ;
But they said that I must linger
  While your vow should bind me here.

"Father, where is Israel's God ?
  Why thus ever hide His face?
Surely He should give approval
  When the sacrifice takes place.

" To a vow should He not hearken ?
  Why not call upon Him now ?
Call, and strike the fatal blow
  To release you from your vow.

" I will raise my eyes to Heaven,
  To that bright celestial sphere,
That my glance may not deter you—
  Quickly, father, do not fear.

" List! the chorus! 'tis the hour
  For the promised sacrifice ;
I am ready ; then hereafter
  Comes the joy of Paradise.

      *   *

"Adah, seek again the spirits
  Of that pure celestial throng ;
Tell them when to earth returning
  To carry this message along.

" Tell them it is a truth that time
  Hides from mortal sight ;
'Tis only seen when first it lives
  Exposed in Heaven's light.

" Errors are human, die with time,
  And unto time belong ;
But all of God's eternity
  Cannot efface a wrong."

Ruth, The Gleaner.

Long years ago, so ancient is the story,
  When Israel abode in Palestine,
Judah, the favored tribe, in princely glory.
  Ruled o'er the land, the first of all the line.

Over Bethlehem their royal standard floated,
  A Lion on a field of azure blue ;
" He who was to come " their standard thus
    denoted,
  And Judah alone reserved, if prophecy were
    true.

Thus Israel rested when Ruth and Naomi came,
  Naomi returning to her native land,
And thus Ruth tells the story which gave her
    life its glory,
  When autumn with its plenty was at hand:

  *

" Long journeyed we from Moab's land,
  O'er dreary waste and shifting sand ;
Looking back, was trouble sore,
  Hope and plenty were all before.
When we reached Judea's plains

The air was sweet with summer rains ;
In the valley far below
  The scene with life was all aglow.
The setting sun's low, mellow ray
  Stretched slanting down the traveled way ;
While purple shadows here and there
  Blended with the ambient air,
And threw a softening, misty haze
  On distant hills and winding ways.
In ever varying light and shade
  The buildings of the city laid ;
In yellow gold its turrets shone,
  Cool shadows o'er its streets were thrown ;
It seemed to us who sought its rest
  A very Mecca for the blest.
Naomi, silent, gazing down
  Upon the valley and the town
Seemed living over what had passed
  Since she beheld that city last.
As memory that past revealed
  Thus did her heart its utterance yield

" ' Oh ! Bethlehem, Oh ! Bethlehem,
  City of peace and rest,
The God of Moses, Thee I Am,
  Has surely called Thee blest.

" ' May I within thy sheltering walls
  But find repose and peace
Until for me the darkness falls
  And light and life shall cease

" ' Here we are tossed as the shifting sand,
  Our life is but a breath,
Which the wisest do not understand
  Since all of it ends in death.

" ' And the wisdom of all in Israel,
  The fathers or those of youth,
From that mysterious silence
  May never wrest the truth.

" ' My sons with their father sleep,
  And the sweetness of earth has flown ;
For who shall say that they live again
  Beyond in the great Unknown.'

" Thus far Naomi's sad lament
I silent heard and silence lent ;
To wake her mind from sorrow's dream
I spake upon another theme :
Naomi, mother, cease to sorrow,
We must care for the tomorrow ;
Night is coming, it is late,
We must reach the entrance gate
Quickly e'er the darkness falls
Or be shut outside the walls.
Then with hastening steps advancing,
Many those who curious glancing,
Yet they gave us courteous greeting,
As the custom was when meeting ;
But of this I need not tell,
We stopped within beside a well,
Where many drew its waters sweet,

Naomi there old friends did meet ;
To others our coming these referred,
Until 'the city was all stirred.'
They came, a thronging multitude'
In various garb and various mood ;
Some, curious only, upon us gazed.
Others in sorrow stood amazed,
And marveled that decree of fate
Which left Naomi desolate.
Her station high, and honored name,
Her kinsman first in Judah's fame,
And all her youth they first recall
Who let this wondering question fall :
' *Is this Naomi?*' As they spoke
Her bitter sorrow all awoke.
'Call me not Naomi, call me Marah ;
For the Lord hath dealt bitterly with me.
Full went I out, and the Lord hath brought me
Home again empty to thee.'
Then one who all her speech had heard
Comforted with gentle word—

  ' Sister, from a loving God
   Life directed is complete ;
  Hope is that all-potent rod
   Which makes the bitter, sweet.

  ' It is the gift of Israel's God,
   A light which beckons on ;
  It never shines upon the past,
   But is the future's dawn.

You are weary, spent and worn,
Rest with me until the morn.'
'Till of weariness divested
In that peaceful home we rested.
Now, being of the Gentile race,
The barriers within this place,
Separating Judah's line,
Were stronger in this land than mine,
Upon this race I had no claim
Save that of my dead husband's name.
Love for Naomi did abound,
And thus through her I favor found '
To gain for us a livelihood,
Naomi keep in cheerful mood.
I needs must glean. I chose the field
Which seemed to most abundant yield ;
Deeming its owner would not care
For scattered grain I gathered there.
At hour of noon with greeting came
The master—Boaz was his name.
Mingling with his maidens I
Hoped unnoticed to pass by,
Knowing not what form of speech
Custom demanded or should teach ;
Watchful the glance he threw around,
Oppressive silence reigned profound,
As when something is amiss ;
Then questioned he, 'Whose damsel's this?'
' From Moab's country the damsel came,
With Naomi ; mine be the blame

If aught is amiss.   She said, I pray
Let me glean among the sheaves today.
Here she has been since the morning broke.'
Thus he who led the reapers spoke.
With sorrow's mist my eyes were dim,
But fearing blame would be on him
Who unto me permission gave,
With full intent to pardon crave,
I raised my eyes to Boaz face ;
What did I see ?   It was the grace
Of Wisdom, Beauty, Strength combined,
A mirror of the heart and mind.
There was a light within his eyes
Which searched through all my heart's disguise.
I raised my hands, my gleanings small
Uplifted held before them all.
I could not speak, there was a spell,
A sense of the invisible.
Have you not felt it ? hearts will fill,
And strangely fast the pulses thrill.
From that mysterious immense,
Outside the utmost bounds of sense,
He touched us both who gave us breath
And something hidden waked from death,
Brief as that glance it bound us fast,
Linking the future and the past ;
It swept the spirit's stringed keys,
They trembled with the melodies
Of love's unspoken symphonies ;
We heard, and in that vibrant sound

The mystic key of life was found.
That same eve ere we reposed
I to Naomi all disclosed.
She spake of what the law had willed,
Of prophecy to be fulfilled ;
Of Israel's race in Bethlehem's land,
Of much I did not understand.
But this alone was clear to me,
Israel's God mine own must be.
Did he not say, ' Under whose wings
Thou art come to trust ?'   Of future things
I pictured happy, bright and fair
If he with me that future share.
Naomi talked—my only prayer
Was for His presence everywhere—
' He called thee daughter ; those who heard
Knew the adoptive right conferred
By he who understood the law
And prophecy's fulfillment saw.
She saw arise from Israel's race
A prince of Judah's line, to grace
A coming throne ; and this of me :
I Am declared 'twas his decree,
A royal Star of Jacob's line,
Linking the human and divine.'
Thus spake Naomi, while I lent
A listening ear to all intent.
While pondering o'er a faith so strange
I slept ; and then there came a change—
I clasped an infant to my breast

As o'er the sandy waste we pressed,
Boaz and I.   'Twas on my mind
That enemies were close behind
Pursuing us to harm the child.
Profanes they were, with hearts defiled ;
We hastened onward ; as we fled
Our footsteps past a field were led.
Therein was one who planted corn ;
That instant on my mind was borne
This form of speech :   Oh, my friend,
We are distressed, assistance lend ;
They come who ask if we have passed,
They follow in our footsteps fast.
If this they wish to know of you
Answer them thus, and answer true—
I saw them pass, it was the morn,
When I was here sowing this corn.
We hastened onward in our flight,
But ere the place was out of sight
I backward glanced ; a vast array
Of armed horsemen filled the way.
As flashed the scimeter and shield,
They halted there beside the field.
But, lo ! in that brief interspace
A wondrous change has taken place—
The God of nature interposed,
The ' Yellow Ray ' His power disclosed ;
Behold the corn grew rank and tall,
The ' Yellow Ray ' had clothed it all ;
In ripened gold its tassels waved.

And by that sign the child was saved. †
I wakened, then, the silvery light
Of Isis shone and filled the night ;
I silent pondered o'er the thought
How beauteous were life's changes wrought ;
Yet marveled that this happy change
Should thus my dreaming thoughts derange.
Long after this, when we were wed,
I told Boaz the dream ; he said :
' In prophecy not all is told ;
When comes the time it will unfold.
Pharoah sought the young child's life ;
In Judah if there should be strife
When comes the prophet of ' I Am ' ;
If Priest or King, or as that Lamb,
Who is the type of innocence,
Eloi grant him that defence
Which is in strength and wisdom bound,
And only in the light is found ;
Who comes as Jacob's Star Divine
Has naught to fear under our mystic sign.
In prophecy of old there calls
Sorrow within this city's walls ;
The voice of weeping, her children dead,
Ramah cannot be comforted.

---

† There is a legend telling that when Joseph and Mary
were fleeing with the young child into Egypt to escape
from Herod they were pursued by Roman soldiers, who
inquired of a man in a field of corn if he had seen them
pass. He replied to them as requested by Mary, and the
soldiers, seeing the ripened corn, naturally supposed that
many days had gone by since they had passed, and pursued them no farther.

If the past the future bind,
Your dream that future has defined.
With Him a year is as a day,
The second Pharoah may be far away.'

    *   *   *   *   *

There is little left to tell ;
Here in Bethlehem we dwell ;
But oft as falls the autumn haze
I wander out among the maize,
Its sweeping waves of yellow gold
A symbol of my story told.
I love the autumn's yellow ray,
Whose beauty covers all decay ;
Its color glows with nature's dawn,
The new life when the old is gone ;
And when the harvest is complete
Boaz brings home a sheaf of wheat ;
And at our outer door it stands.
A type of plenty in the land.
The poor all know that in this sign
Wisdom and charity combine ;
And these. he says, are Heaven-sent.
And in their power Omnipotent.

    *   *   *   *   *   *

Oft as my babe around me plays
My dream returns with night's soft haze ;
The child by enemies oppressed,
Waking I clasp him to my breast,
And pray that old-time prophecy
May not refer to mine or me.

In Yellow Robes I'm always dressed,
Because it is Boaz' request ;
But most because I used to glean,
I love this robe of yellow sheen."

The Signet of Solomon.

Afar o'er Persia's burning sand
The ruins of a city stand ;
Where soft Ulali's waters creep
Its princely glory sank to sleep ;
O'er what remains of palace wall
The serpent and the lizard crawl ;
Shushan a remnant of decay
And Persia's glory passed away ;
The stars look down like eyes of fate
Upon that land made desolate.
But at the time of which I write
It glowed with splendour and delight ;
Such as there was no rival known
Since Solomon sat on the throne ;
For all the treasures Cyrus gained
Were here by Persian kings retained ;
Enriched with spoils from every land,
And all were at the king's command.
Oh ! happy king, to want for naught.
And yet some things cannot be bought ;
Who lives today, thus being bid,
But would not do as Vashti did ?
But royalty must power command,

The queen is banished from the land ;
No more is seen her lovely face,
Esther, the Jewess, takes her place.
And now the fast declining sun
Shines down the terraced walk upon ;
A fountain gushes there in play
And foliage heavy shrouds the way.
But little from the path aside,
Where roses bloom and lilies hide,
Two Persian maids in idle mood
There revel in the solitude ;
One plays upon the lute's soft strings,
And sorrowfully thus she sings :

"Vashti, the beautiful, where dost thou wander,
   Over the palace the darkness has come ;
Vashti, in sorrow o'er thy fate I ponder,
   Where hast thou vanished, where is thy home,
   Vashti, banished queen, where now, is thy
      home ?

" Vashti, beloved one, ever we sigh for thee
   Fairer than the lilies by the river side ;
Graceful, lovely, shall we never more behold
   The gem of Persia, its light and its pride ;
   Vashti, banished queen, ever our love and our
      pride ?

Vashti, beloved, dim are our eyes with tears,
   Tremulous our voices while we sing ;
Stars of Heaven guide thee through the coming
      years,

To thee our love shall ever cling.
Vashti, departed one, to thee our love shall
    ever cling.

Hush! Seppho, let thy lute be still,
    And cease to thus lament ;
The stars decree our fate and will
    The way our lives are sent.
Shamar, the watchful, walks without the court,
And he would to this new queen report
Without delay the matter of your song,
No more to Vashti do we now belong ;
And this late favorite would hardly like to hear
The praise of Vashti sounded in her ear.
Be wise ; do not the past retrace,
The present is our only time and place ;
Uncertain is the future as the past,
The favor of the court is none too sure to last.
This Esther, too, is beautiful and bright,
Full of grace and sweetness that delight
The senses and the heart ; and kind intent
Beams o'er her face, as if she meant
To give to all that generous meed
Of sympathy which the less favored need.
The name she bears denotes a star ;
It is a happy omen.   From afar
'Tis said she comes ; and of her race
No one here knows their abiding place.
'Tis said the king, when they were wed,
Designed to have a banquet spread ;
A feast most royal in design,

That he might thus her friends define ;
And when he told t'was for her sake
She said, " Let no such thought awake ;
An orphan I, and have no friends,
Save on'y such as Heaven sends."
Then, pitying her, he was content,
Unheeding of what Shamar meant,
When once he called her by her name,
Hadassah, from the Hebrew came—
That captive race within this land—
And sometimes things like this are planned.
But, Seppho, if I do unfold
What I have seen, and you are told,
Will you be faithful to the trust
Until your heart shall turn to dust ?
The Zendavesta—kiss the book,
And may the Fire God on you look.
Know then that I have seen the Jew
Named Mordecai, oft in view.
He loiters 'round as if by chance,
But most of all his watchful glance
Is toward the Queen's apartments bent
As if on interview intent.
Once o'er the court as Shamar walked
He and this Mordecai talked.
'Tis he who keeps the inner gate
Where all the king's attendants wait.
Sad and anxious was his look,
And Shamer his instructions took,
Then to the Queen's apartments bent

His footsteps, hastily he went.
And save but I no one discerned
When Shamar with the queen returned.
Wonder filled her face and eyes,
Which flashed with eager, pleased surprise ;
No stranger was he to the queen,
But as a dear friend might have been ;
And what they spake may I repeat
When Ormuzd and Ahiram meet ?
And since that time may never come,
I see no need to now be dumb ;
For, Seppho, what I tell to you
Shall be as though I never knew.
It seems there was a murderous plot
By Bigthan and by Teresh wrought
To strike the king from off the throne,
The wrong to Vashti to atone.
To Vashti's kin they did belong,
And thus they thought to right the wrong.
Their purpose Mordecai learned,
To Esther then his footsteps turned,
Acquainted her with their design
That she might give the king a sign,
And say by him the matter found
So to his honor t'would resound.
These walls enclose us in a nest,
But I did chance to learn the rest.
The matter laid before the king
Was compassed by a little thing ;
They both were guards, and one did boast

That he was absent from his post.
The matter bare, no chance to flee,
They both were hanged upon a tree.
I doubt not he who keeps the gate
Will sometime fill a chair of state,
If this he by design intends
The queen will aid, for they are friends ;
And she is of the Hebrew race,
Or my guess is much out of place."

The speaker ceased, and Seppho,
  With merry gesture cried,
" Persis, you surely have knowledge
  That reaches far and wide ;
But, Persis, you are a babbler,
  A babbler and no mistake,
And if you had to cease your talk
  Your heart would surely break.
What matter if Queen Esther
  Belonged to the Hebrew race ?
Vashti could not have chosen one
  To better fill her place.
[Tho' I say it who loved the Persian queen,
  For her heart was full of grace.]
With all your knowledge, Persis,
  You are not overwise ;
Methinks sometime the king and you
  Will meet with a great surprise.
In the land from whence the Hebrews came
  They had a king of their own,

But Persia captured their treasures
    And Solomon's golden throne
Is the glory of Sushan palace
    Where Solomon's wisdom is known.
And they tell that in that city—
    Jerusalem was its name—
Where the Hebrew God was worshipped,
    A Temple by magic came.
Three workmen only laid the plans,
    And one was a master mind,
Direct d by the Hebrew God,
    And all their plans combined,
So that when the timbers all were cut
    And the stones to design referred,
It grew to place in a single night,
    And never a sound was heard
Of cutting timber or shaping rock,
    But only a magic word.
It is said that when Darius was king
    Such wisdom therein he discerned
That he questioned long a captive Prince
    But nothing from him learned,
Save that "truth was mighty and would prevail,"
    Or words to that effect ;
And they say that Darius was so abashed
    He could only say, ' Quite correct,'
And he entertained for the captive Prince
    Thereafter a great respect.
Of the mysteries of their craftsmen
    Never a sign would he give ;

But he said that rather than be untrue
  He would sooner die than live.
'Tis said that before he left the king
  His horoscope he cast,
And told of a long-forgotten vow
  Darius had made in the past,
Concerning some holy vessels
  Left over at Babylon,
Which he thought to return to them again
  But never caused it done.
When the king much honor on him conferred
  He returned to his native land,
And the Persians study ever since
  Those mysteries to understand.
These Hebrews worship but one God,
  And they claim to be his sons ;
The only Fire-God that they know
  Burns up the wicked ones,
And something that's left of them after that
  With the evil genii runs.
With such we little have to do
  Who live from day to day,
And measure our lives the whole way through
  By what the stars shall say.
But what I mean to tell you, Persis,
  Will set your mind at rest,
If such a matter be possible
  With your knowledge unconfessed.
Queen Esther is of royal blood,
  To Solomon's house allied ;

She is the light of the Hebrew race
   And all their joy and pride.
The glow of the diamond is in her name,
   As it shines in the darkest night,
Peerless above a doubt or blame,
   Estarah, "A Star of Light."

     Shamar comes ; let us retire ;
     His eyes are like the Sacred Fire
     The priests aflame forever keep,
     He never lets them close in sleep.

   *   *   *   *   *   *

In sorrow and sadness came the queen's maidens,
   And thus the cause they disclosed :
" Over the city a sorrow has fallen,
   Where once only joy had reposed.

" Estarah, beloved, darkened is the sunlight,
   Over the palace the shadows now fall ;
The Hebrews are robed in garments of mourning,
   Sackcloth and ashes are over them all.

"But little removed from the shade of the palace,
   Near the gate where he waited in trust,
Weeping and wailing in sorrow and anguish
   Mordecai sits in the dust.

" The Ark, where tne law of Moses reposes
   They carried this morn through the street—
A symbol of death—in silence oppressive
   It was swathed in a black winding sheet.

" Perhaps 'tis a plague that has fallen upon us,
　And the poor feel the touch of its breath ;
For the sackcloth and ashes that darken the city
　Only come with the shadow of death."

　Then Esther's heart beat fast with dread
　While thus their lamentations spread
　　　These scenes before her gaze ;
　Alas ! what had her people done,
　She marveled much and thought upon
　　　With sorrow and amaze.
　"Oh ! maidens, gather the garments white—
　Spare only my royal robes of light—
　　　That we may here command,
　These I request that they shall wear ;
　Hatach, give them o'er with care
　　　Into Mordecai's hand ;
　And say to him that I, the queen,
　Would fain know what the Hebrews mean.
　　　If they are ought oppressed
　The king the matter will surely hear,
　Kind is his heart, they need not fear ;
　　　He will set the thing at rest."

　　Slow of step Hatach returned,
　　　A copy within his hand
　　Of a decree the king had given
　　　Which the wicked Haman planned.

" Oh, Queen," said he, " I have seen the Jew,
　This copy will disclose to you ;
　A slaughter of your people planned,

Of all who dwell within this land.
Mordecai this message sends—
On you the Hebrews' hope depends—
'Tis that you go before the king
And for them intercession bring.''

    *   *   *

Then Esther's cheek grew pale with fear,
As one who sees death drawing near,
    Her heart with anguish filled ;
'' Oh ! back to Mordecai go
And ask him if he does not know
A law the king has willed ;
    That when he sits upon his throne,
Within the inner court, 'tis known
    That none may enter there
Save only those for whom he calls ;
That honor to the queen ne'er falls,
    And this is my despair ;
For those who of themselves intrude
And find him not in gracious mood
    The sceptre to extend,
There stands his law, it needs no test,
It covers me with all the rest,
    Death is the certain end.
Oh ! Hatach, tell him I will pray
Unto Jehovah night and day,
    And that my maids and I
On beds of ashes will repose,
But young and strong my life blood flows
    And I do fear to die.''

    *   *   *   *   *

Mordecai then returned
These words to Esther, and they burned
The doubt and fear from out her heart :
" Know, then, you are of us a part ;
If this decree shall take its course
The queen shall not escape its force ;
And if thou now shalt hold thy peace
Thou and thy father's house shalt cease ;
Jehovah from another place
Will send deliverance and grace.
Who knows if you your fears dismiss
You are come to the throne for a time like this."

* * * * * *

When selfish thought is thrust aside
Then mortal life is deified ;
The path of love and duty trod
Will lead the soul straight up to God ;
And swiftly born or slowly wrought,
Noble deeds are never bought.
'Tis said that all of nature's fear
In Heaven's gaze will disappear ;
That when the soul is pure and white
The darkness cannot cloud its light ;
It is a gift of God's design,
A symbol of his light divine ;
Whate'er its time of mortal birth
Its radiance flashes o'er the earth,
And shines while Empires rise and fall,
While Time the roll of Centurys call,
Its light eternal will unfold

And shine when all the "stars grow cold."
    Thus was the soul of Esther born
    To "walk in beauty," like the morn.

    *   *   *   *   *   *

While peaceful she reposed that night
Strange and wild her fancy's flight ;
Dreaming, she left the woman's court,
Nor of her absence gave report.
Passing through the palace halls
She stood without its shining walls ;
Nor sentry nor the inner guard
E'er sought her footsteps to retard.
Indeed, they seemed to see her not
Or know the gates did ope and shut.
The moon's soft light around her fell,
Through it she walked invisible.
No conscious sense alert to guide
She started toward the river side.
When far outside the city's gate
The path she trod grew intricate ;
It led her o'er an eminence,
And jutting cliffs without defence ;
Then winding down the river side,
O'er heavy rock and fissures wide.
With step light as an antelope
She passed adown the hillside slope.
Thick grew the lilies there and rank
So that they covered all the bank ;
Their perfume, like a mist of light,
Was wafted on the breeze of night ;

Their leaves and blossoms interlace
And fold the queen in their embrace ;
They kiss her cheek with fond caress,
As though they only meant to bless,
And say, "Oh, Queen, you are one of us,
And loving you we greet you thus."
She did not tarry or delay
But through the lilies made her way.
In murmured tones and whispering
Ulali's waters gently sing ;
The noisy waves they drowned deep,
So that the night should silence keep ;
As though it were disloyalty
If Persia's queen disturbed should be ;
And marveled much what wondrous thing
The presence of the queen should bring.
She glances round, then hesitates,
And, listening, attentive waits.
There stands a rock ; a strange device
Is graven upon it ; once or twice
With lifted hands upon it pressed
She sought to move it from its rest.
In vain ; she has no key to guide ;
But as she looks it swings aside,
As though t'was easy to submit,
Someone inside had opened it.
She knows him well ; a man renowned,
With curious gaze he glanced around ;
"'Twas but the noises of the night,
No one is near but the Upright."

She answered, "Count me one of those
Who follow where the Upright goes."
He saw her not, nor heard her speak,
Yet sudden pallor blanched his cheek
With sense of mystery and fear,
As though a wandering soul was near.
Beyond, the way was dim and dark,
Save but of light a single spark
From out the inner cavern thrown
Told the place from which it shown.
Still by unconscious sense impelled,
She entered, and this scene beheld—
An Altar built of rock-hewn stone,
The black of mourning o'er it thrown;
The Ark of God upon it placed;
A soft light shown, subdued and chaste
Over the Ark and sacred law
And upon it arranged she saw
　The compasses and square.
　　Upon the circling stones around
　　Sat figures who in black were gowned,
　A conclave of despair.
　　Then one arose, and thus he spake:
　　"Brothers, let your hearts awake
　　And let us plead for Israel's sake—
　　　Jehovah hear our prayer.

　　　Oh! God, All-powerful, Great I Am,
　　　　Forever clothed in light,
　　　Deliver us from evil ones　　　᾽
　　　　And guide our steps aright;

Encompassed by our enemies,
In Thee our only trust,
Let Thy light shine upon us,
And raise us from the dust."

While thus as Mordecai prayed,
Esther, wondering and afraid,
Thought to make her presence known,
And for her coming to atone :
She looked upon him face to face,
No recognition there could trace
Nor look of stern surprise.
" He wills that I shall here abide,
And learn what they tonight decide
Ere death shall close my eyes."

*   *   *   *   *   *

" I have a measure to disclose,"
Said Mordecai : " In it flows
The blood of honored sacrifice,
And Esther's life may be its price ;
'Tis all our hope ; if she will plead
We may escape this time of need.
But now your counsel I beseech
Upon a matter that doth reach
Unto the hearts of all.
Within the sacred Ark there lies,
Hidden away where curious eyes
And profane may not fall,
Signet of Solomon, whose fame
I learned to Ahasuerur came ;

I chance to know that he did see
And knows the Signet's mystery
    And will regard its power.
If his favor she fails to reach
The Signet will have power of speech
    In that momentous hour.
If you will thus decide tonight
Esther shall take the 'Star of Light'
    That it may greet his eyes.
Some cubes are black and some are white,
They tell of darkness and of light ;
Who has the power to read aright
    Will find their lessons wise."

     *   *   *   *   *

Momentous silence overcast
The fleeting moments as they passed ;
    Thus was the edict read :
"No clouds obscure the stars tonight,
Jehovah yet may raise upright
    The Hebrews from the dead."
Then all grew dim and far away
And Esther woke to light of day ;
She pondered o'er the wondrous chase
Her fancy led her, and the place ;
To be a mirage of the mind
Most perfectly it was designed ;
And what was woven while she slept
Her waking sense securely kept.

   *   *   *   *   *   *

Swift passed the measured hours away
Unto that dread, momentous day.
The queen arrayed her as a bride
Whose loveliness was glorified
By richest royal robes of state
That could her beauty consecrate.
A gown of shimmering white she wore,
Its lustrous surface covered o'er
In tracing of unique design,
With costly gems that intertwine ;
In emerald stones and ruby, glows
The green of foliage and the rose ;
And here and there the amethyst
Shines through a cloud of lace-like mist.
From where the lovely lilies bent
The diamonds flashing light was sent ;
And under where the stamens curl
The surface all was sown with pearl ;
Over her shoulders lightly thrown
A royal purple sash was shown,
To half conceal and half disclose
The loveliness which 'neath it glows ;
Her face a dream of beauty rare,
Fairest of all where all were fair.

The queen in beauty thus arrayed
Looked to the east and softly prayed—
    " Jehovah, God of Israel,
      Divine Eternal King,
    I to Thine Omnipotent power

For intercession cling.
O'er all the earth Thou hast command,
  And those who here abide
May not stay Thy righteous hand
  Nor ever from Thee hide.
Thy people, captive Hebrews here,
  Are by this edict slain ;
If Thou dost not deliver us
  Then all our hope is vain.
Thou knowest in these royal robes
  My heart has naught of pride ;
They mock the anguish of my soul,
  Be Thou my strength and guide ;
And when I come before the king
  Oh ! soften Thou his heart,
That it may cling to me, and say,
  'Oh, bid her not depart.' "

Flashed the sunlight on the palace,
  Far away it reached the sight,
O'er the glittering sands reflecting
  Undulating waves of light.
Where you entered at the gateway
  Soft and cool the shadows creep,
Silent as the fated palace
  Where the princess fell asleep.
All the guards, like living statues
  Motionless, in silence stand ;
None may here intrude or enter

Only at the king's command.
  Further to enforce this warning,
    When the king was on his throne
Black was draped o'er all the arches
    That death's signal should be known.
Those who came to ask his favor
    Tarried in the outer court,
And those who with urgent message
    Should be called to make report.
Through the corridor there echoes
    Sound of footsteps soft and low,
O'er the tassellated marble
    Nearer come and stronger grow.
Glancing curiously, and watchful,
    With intent and listening ear,
Rigid stand the guards, and anxious,
    Wondering who should thus draw near.
She comes with her attendant maids,
    " Esterah, Star of Light ;"
The guards behold her with amaze
    Nor question of her right.
They knew her peril and their own.
    But she was Persia's queen ;
Between the two did duty call
    For them to intervene ?
Brief time had they to weigh the thought,
    With dismay overcome,
Before her stately loveliness
    They silent stood and dumb.
But at the inner entrance

A Persian soldier stood ;
With drawn sword he barred the way,
  " Oh dare not to intrude ;
Admitted here without request
  'Tis death to you and I ;
I fear it not, but you are far
  Too beautiful to die.."
" Heaven alone our fates decide,
  Death ever walks unseen—
Your duty done—now stand aside—
  I am Persia's queen !"
The silken curtains tremble
  As with uplifted hands
She parted them and entered,
  Before the king she stands.

He looked upon her, flushed his face
  With anger and surprise ;
Was this another Vashti
  Who his command defies?

But all her grace and loveliness
  Unto his heart appealed ;
Perhaps regret for Vashti lost
  His love for Esther sealed.

While looking thus upon her
  A ray of sunlight came,
It covered her with radiance bright
  And glory all aflame.

The flashing of the emerald,
  The ruby's ruddy shade,
The amethyst and diamond
  In vivid lightning played.
They cast their bright, transparent light
  O'er the beauty of her face ;
Her eyes, like stars through prison bars,
  Appealed to him for grace.

She raised her jeweled hand and touched
  The royal crown she wore ;
He knew her meaning, but the crown
  Another message bore—

A wondrous Star, and thus it spake
  To Ahasuerus eyes ;
" From these five points no vows revoke,
  Nor hide them in disguise."

It was enough ; no harm could come
  To whom this Signet bore ;
The starry fame of Esther's name
  Shall live for evermore.

  *   *   *   *   *

And that is how it came to pass,
  Though but to few 'twas known—
For Esther ever silence kept,
  As the Sphynx of graven stone —
That the Signet of Solomon appealed
  To the King on the Persian throne.

"If a Man Die, Shall he Live Again?"

Rabbi Ben Ezra sat within his study. From the leaves of the parchment before him he was intent upon copying texts to guide his pupils in their morrow's task ; to each his separate work.

The failing light admonished him that day was done, and ceasing to write he sought the open window.

Far below the streets of Jerusalem,— narrow and ever winding in their course seemed as a maze of tangled threads.

Few were the travelers ; the traffic of the day had ceased, and fast that shade descended of which is born the twilight and the night, and as it o'er the city spread its misty wings, Rabbi Ben Ezra thus in his own thought communed:

" Our heathen rulers call this hour ' the twilight of the Gods.' Much knowledge have they; even their poesy is copied from the sacred Word of Judah's prophet."

" Oh ! that the Great ' I Am,' would remember now the remnant of His chosen people, and send the promised One to restore our place and nation."

"Daily do these Romans profane His Holy Name, and mock us in our helpless state.

Surely the records cannot err, for ever faithfully they have been kept, and in the prophecy's fulfillment our promised King must soon appear; and yet, Elijah first shall come again. Then will "Judah's Lion," clothed with splendour, follow in his footsteps, from before whose royal power the Roman Eagle shall depart, and wing its way unto another eyrie; the "House of David" once more reign, and Israel's God among His people dwell, and in His "Holy Temple."

"But now the darkness thickens to a sombre shade. 'Tis time the youth, Joseph Akiba, had returned."

"He is a faithful lad; Caiaphas need not fear to entrust with him the copy."

"Almost I love him as my son, and if I still abide on earth when comes our King, and my plea will avail, he shall obtain an honored place."

While thus the Rabbi pondered, the youth was hastening through the narrow streets with eager and impatient step, to reach the Rabbi's presence. His face was all aglow with light of some suppressed emotion; entering within the open door, low bowed he in salutation; then before Ben Ezra spoke, thus eager he began:

"Oh! Rabbi, I have seen Him; the Youth whose wisdom did confuse the understanding of the doctors of the law, within the Holy Temple.

"It was at the well, where in the noon-day heat I rested — I doubt not you do know the spot. 'Tis where there stands a cedar high, with branches spreading wide, like unto those on Lebanon's great mountain. Centuries ago it must have taken root, for it has grown so that it shades the waters o'er almost to darkness.

"'Tis a delightful spot. There was I resting when He came; near to mine own age is He and it is easy to discern that poverty was in His home, and that by labour did He earn His bread; but such a kingly grace, and withal modest mien, such comeliness of form and face of beauty might the Seraphs wear, for I have never yet beheld such loveliness, even in all Jerusalem.

"Fair as a lily, was He; His eyes blue as the azure of the sky when the storm-clouds have passed away and left the beauty and the light of heaven there.

"His hair held all the rays of sunshine, from golden tint to amber shade; so strangely mingled was it that I can scarce describe it; but in that history of David, the great King, which late you taught us, He was so like that I could fancy David, thus in his youth appeared.

" Rabbi, my heart went out to Him, and as I greeting gave, He stayed His steps, and lingering there with me we converse held. And Rabbi, I must tell you that of which He spake while yet His every word I do remember. I told Him who I was, and then I spoke of you, my teacher, wise beyond all others in Jerusalem, and knowing all the law.

" But Rabbi, how exceedingly dull I must have ever been, for I have nothing learned compared to knowledge He has gained.

" His thought is like that fabled alchemy of old ; His wisdom can transmute the simplest things of earth into eternal truths. I chanced to speak concerning that doctrine of eternal life which the Pharisees so strictly teach.

" Perchance," said He, " they study Nature's ways."

Then answered I : " You do not surely know the Pharisees. Nature to them is very small indeed, and nothing worth ; but they are very urgent in the law, and study to be seen of men, that thus they may be deemed the sanctified, and holy of the earth. But do you to me impart what you have learned of Nature's ways, and how this doctrine she observes for I would learn of this." Then, Rabbi, thus He spake:

" Have your eyes never yet beheld that which Nature in ever-moving silence builds? It is not a blind force and dumb, but an eternal language which in continued action ever is expressed."

"Nature is the Heaven-born architect Jehovah gave unto the world, to teach mankind. The earth is her great trestle-board, and the Creator's vast designs she traces there before the eyes of men, that all may look and ponder. Thus by immortal truths, the lessons of eternity are taught unto earth's children; these she imparts to lead them into light."

"She never errs, though hers is a momentous work, and grand beyond compare."

"In Paradise Jehovah hides that hour-glass which shall measure Time; but to us on earth He gives the passing hours as from eternity they fall."

"The doors of Time, are thus ever-present, and are ever open wide, for Time is Nature's work-shop."

"The days and years are pliant tools within her skilful hands.

"She holds the centuries as the plastic clay; she moulds them into history, and then folds them away. And where they thus repose, sealed fast; this barrier is inscribed:

"I Am the Past."

"Her lessons easy to be understood, if we but find the key. The seasons each do come in their appointed time. In silence each its work performs; in silence then depart."

"These are the lessons that they teach:"
"The Spring-time's green is Nature's resurrection robe. Summer is that resurrection's fruitage in all its glorious promise, throbbing with the burden of the life it bears. Then follows Autumn, glowing with the yellow shade of fruition falling to decay; but soft and slow of step this shadow comes, and over all of fading life is thrown a veil of beauty."

"Look how the leaves ever drink in the light, and ere they fall to earth, behold how that light has transformed them, clothing them with all its beauteous shades, and covering them with glory."

"It is as though they laugh, and say, why should we fear decay? Are we not far more beautiful for the life we cast away."

"In Winter is her lesson given of that brief space, in which the body, when from the soul and spirit freed, will rest in its repose."

"'Tis then that Heaven sends its veil of white to cover Nature's face; but deep within her breast the music of eternal life is flowing, and when she breathes upon the land again, the green of life appears."

He plucked a blade of grass, and asked of me: "Can thy wise teacher but create a shade like this?"

"Yea," said I: "It is a simple thing to do." He takes the colors known, and mixes the yellow and the blue."

Then did He say: "The lesson thus is brought to view. Blue is a symbol of eternal truth; this, with the yellow, symbol of decay, combined, these teach us that in them united, we eternal life may find."

"But without the aid of these two colors, we never can produce the green, save only when it it is with poison mingled."

"Thus is the other lesson taught; that we cannot impart eternal life; nor yet can we create its symbol save with the poison of mortality and death to enter in."

Then spake I to Him of David, saying that when the tomb was opened wherein the body had reposed, the King lay there in fleshy form and life-like sleep, but lo! to stone his body had been changed.

"A miracle," the Rabbis said, "for so had David wrote in prophecy, in words like unto these: Thou wilt not suffer thine Holy One to see corruption."

Then did the Youth say unto me: "Be not deceived; surely the Rabbis err. It was Nature's gift of love; she interposed her mighty power before decay, and gave what immortality she could bestow unto a form of clay."

"Rabbi, more I could not say; thou knowest that the life of David was not from error free, and knowing this, I could not declare and say he was that Holy One of God. Yet strange it seems the Rabbis thus should err."

After brief silence interposed, He, from the over-spreading cedar, plucked a branch, and thus discoursed:

"Here is the emblem of a truth that lives since lives the world."

* "The cedar never knows decay."

"In living green it ever stands; from the snowy bosom of the earth, it lifts its icy hands; it shades the hoar-frost from its head, and pointing to the sky, symbol of immortality, says naught shall ever die."

"It knows no change, even where change is rife. Green is the symbol of eternal life."

"Much cedar wood they used within the Holy Temple."

"Yea," said I, "but Herod knows not this significance of which you speak."

"Herod I have never known;" He made reply: "My thoughts did wander back to Solomon the wise, and to the Tyrian workman."

Then it was that I inquired of Him: "Hast thou seen the Temple?"

"Yea, at the Feast of the Passover, I was there," He answered me.

"Tell me," I said, "Art thou He who questioned the Rabbis, and spake of Moses' law as one who had been strictly taught?"

---

* It is a well known fact that cedar-wood is indestructible, save by fire. There is in the British Museum a specimen of cedar wood taken from the palace of Nimrod ; it is known to be 3,000 years old.

"Yea," said He; "I did ask them questions."

"They are wise men," said I.

"Wisdom is old; older far than they;" He made reply.

Then questioned I: "Who taught you of these truths of which you have discoursed?"

Long He kept silence, as if pondering; then as one by doubt oppressed, He answered me— "*My Father.*"

"A learned, and an honored one among that sect, the Caballists, surely must your Father be."

"I have heard that in mysterious hidden places; in the lowes valleys and on the highest mountains they do meet and study mysteries of science, of which the outer world may never know; and it is thought they strictly teach this doctrine of immortal life; for when they lay to rest within the sepulchre, one of their number gone, they each a branch of evergreen cast into his last resting-place."

Then, Rabbi; sadly did he give dissent.

"None of this my father knows. He is a carpenter; in yonder village toils he for his daily bread. until the day is done; his nights are passed in rest."

"The Father of whom I learn is one I find at nights when my body sleeps."

Then questioned I: "What mystery is yours?"

" Flushed His lovely face, as of one innocent, who is accused of wrong ; and thus appealing to me, said : " Oh ! tell me if you can, for as yet I cannot see it clearly, and I cannot divine its meaning. Alas ! it is a crown of sorrow that ever drives the sunshine from my heart."

" Here in Nazareth have I always spent my days, save for that journey to Jerusalem ; and of other lands naught have I ever seen."

" Know you if in any country there is built a city most glorious in its beauty ; one whose streets are laid with purest, brightest gold; whose gates are of a milk white pearl ; whose walls are built of precious stones of many colors, which shine like gems of light, and flash afar the radiance of their glory ; so that the eye can never follow them ; and over all the city there shines a great white light, before whose glorious brightness yonder sun would fade away."

I answered : " Nay, I never heard of it. There may be such in Egypt ; that land wherein the Hebrews were made slaves. I have learned they builded for that people great pyramids of stone, and temples for their heathen gods. They also searched and found those who were skilful to execute in figures, and engrave in stone ; then carried they a great large stone into the desert place, and of it was carved a head and face like unto humankind ; the body prone upon the sands, as it

were a mighty giant resting there, whose
eyes forever watched the world; but ere
they finished it, Jehovah sent the desert wind
to heap the sands of the lost Ocean there, and
so they buried it; and only but the eyes of it
do now look out to mock all Egypt's greatness.

"But of this city you would know; I do
much doubt if Egypt ever yet bestowed such
treasures on a city in that land; too much they
fear the waters called the Nile, would sometime rise and swallow it."

"In my own mind I am assured that never
yet was built a city in this world containing
more of richness and of beauty than our own
Jerusalem when God yet visited His people;
but even it, in all its glory had none of this
which you describe."

"Then," spake He: "It is a mystery I do
not understand; but truthfully I speak when I
do say that every night I live in such a city.
Its beauties and its pleasures all are real; it
seems to be my home. There One who dwells
within that light, teaches me of wisdom and of
truth, before whose living power the wisdom
and the truths of earth are as reflections of a
light cast into a dark place; and yet I seem to
have known it all before in ages long since
past."

"Confused the memory I retain; but ever to
my waking sense the echoes of its music and

its beauties waken words like unto these—
though words can tell it not:

    "A glorious sea, whose waters shine,
      With crystal beauty all divine,
    And there ten thousand voices sing,
      In praise of some eternal king,
    And of a blessed One, the slain —
      Who sometime over all shall reign.
    But ever as I leave its gates,
      Regretful of my loss—
    Upon my path, in darkness falls
      The shadow of a cross."

"When I waken I am the carpenter's son, and I am here in Nazareth."

"Since first I come to understanding of the things of life, I have seen this vision, or whatsoever it may be. As I older grow it seems to deepen to a greater truth; the end I know not; sometimes I do fear."

Rabbi, He was sad, and troubled in heart and from His tender eyes sorrow looked out as though the soul within had lost its way, and cried aloud for light.

Then love and reverence in my heart awoke, and I, to comfort him; replied: "Perchance you do but dream." Not heeding me He said; "Green is the wall's foundation stone; the sixth is like unto blood, and the twelfth a blue."

"There was I told the green foundation stone did typify eternal life, the upper one of blue,

eternal truth, and the central stone of red
which bound these two did typify the blood of
sacrifice by which that eternal truth and that
eternal life were bought."

"Today I found their likeness." And from
His bosom He drew forth three jewels: Jaspar,
Sardius, and Amethyst, they were.

"Take them," He said, but when He dropped
them in my hand, they all to dust did fall.

Seeing His proffered gift thus strangely fade,
His face took on a sadder shade:

We parted then, and this was His farewell:
"Eloi grant thee peace; and if I sometime find
that city of the night, Joseph Akiba, you shall
share with me its light."

And sorrowing with the memory of that
scene, Joseph, upon his folded arms hid his
face and wept. The moon long since had risen
and now it threw its mellow light within the
room. Rabbi Ben Ezra, strangely moved,
long silence kept. When he spoke it was to
say:

"Son, didst thou find Caiaphas and bring
with you the record?"

"Yea, Rabbi, I had quite forgotten it."

"And Joseph, you are still very young, your
heart is tender, and easily is moved. As for
this youth of whom you tell, I fear He is a
dreamer, though where He learned the truths
He thus expounded, is quite another matter.

" That is what I would speak of," Joseph interposed. "Surely you remember that the learned
doctors said He knew the law, and could in
truth interpret it, and some who listened, said
He knew far more than they; though of that
matter, be it far from me to say, who know so
little."

" But Rabbi, for one moment ponder; might
it not be He is that Prophet come again? Elias
who was of old ; you have taught us that the
time was near at hand, and in this youth's form
and garb, might not Elias now appear ?"

"Would that I could hope it," reverently
Ben Ezra spoke. " But the soul of Elias come
again, will live strong and mature, and needs
not slowly to unfold ; nor will it be of soft and
tender mold, full of dreams and visions of a
shadow city ; but stern and strong to execute
the judgment of Jehovah."

Malachi writes : "The wicked then shall be
as the stubble of the field and shall be
burned with fire, so that under Judah's feet
they will be trod as ashes -- thus shall our
heathen rulers perish."

Once more does Joseph plead : "Then Rabbi,
think again for but one moment, and answer my
appeal. May it not be He is perchance the
"Shiloh," that promised Prince of Peace? If
you could but see Him."

"Vain is thy thought; dost thou not remember that Judah's King will come of David's house, in fitting royal splendour? In Bethlehem he will be born: No, speak not of that fabled star, the Gentile Kings did follow from that heathen land, where fire is worshipped as the God of Light, and where the stars are all the Urim and the Thummin that they know. How should the Persians learn this of Jehovah, when only those from Abraham descended merit the favor to be called His chosen ones?"

"And if perchance it was revealed to them — which Eloi himself forbid — what came of it?"

"They took the little knowledge they had gained to Herod's ears, and of him inquired where they should find this new-born King. Surely you do know the rest. Sad was the story of the "Star of Bethlehem." Methinks I yet can hear the cry of twenty thousand infants slain to build a footstool for King Herod's throne. Ramah, weeping and mourning for her children, and would not be comforted because they were not."

"If that slaughter told the death of Judah's promised King, then is there naught in all of prophecy. The years in silence pass, in silence hold the truth, whate'er it be."

"My son, be not thus led astray; as for these Nazarenes, they are among the outcast, poor, and despised. 'Tis well that you should now

forget this Youth, for He is but a Nazarene
thou art a Prince of Judah."

             *   *

*   *   *   *   *   *

Passing are the years: Judah divided, seek-
ing power and place, vainly cavilled o'er the
letter of the law, and in their bitter disputations
was lost its intent and its spiritual truth.
But most earnestly they questioned of the
life beyond, so that they were at strife among
themselves. There were those who claimed the
resurrection of the body and the soul; those
differing denied to both that hope, saying:

"The mystery beyond the tomb was not a
mystery, but a vast blank of nothingness."

Mockingly they questioned: "What and
whence is this immortality you claim?"
"Where, and by wha· process is it held allied
unto the clay of which the body is?" "What is
its form and essence?"

"Dead are all the Fathers; dead is Abraham,
and all the prophets, turned to dust and ashes;
where is now the place of their abode? Oh!
point it out to us that we may see and know,
and thus believe, and thus also learn where
and how we too may live forever. Then would
the others thus reply in words like unto these:

"If of your wise men there is one who can
devise an eye that will give sight. an ear that
will give hearing, a brain that will produce a

thought, then will we say that these come not of an immortal power, and will not to immortality return."

"And yet perchance ye wise, who do deny the truth, will tell us what it is ye call the soul?"

"It is not that thought known as the mind, for the mind is but the reflection of the soul upon the brain. Neither is the mind, (or call it the spirit, if ye will) dependent on the brain; as ye would say, for the brain is ever being worn away, and thus destroyed, and then again renewed with forces new and strange; just as the body lives, so lives the brain; whereas the mind is a vast storehouse, ever retaining and ever locking up what it has found, and there it ever is from time long past, and at the thought's command. If the mind lived only with the brain, and with it died, then would the mind die ever, and forget the past."

"Surely the brain is but the instrument which to the body does convey the message from the mind."

"Yet only give more hours to study and perchance you yet can tell us how the soul is to the body bound, and by what process and what power it is annihilated."

"If it is not the link that binds man to his Creator, then it is nothing worth, and has no place nor part, here, or in the hereafter."

"Ye likewise well do know, and have not denied, that in all the realm of Nature and of Nature's God, there is no final death; death is the mask that change doth wear." "The form may pass away; it but resolves into another element, and ever lives for aye."

"Do not even thus the heathen believe, who write:

"There lives this truth in life's bright light,
    As in the grave's dark shade;
The Gods, themselves, cannot destroy,
    Aught they have ever made."

*   *   *   *

Joseph Akiba, grown to manhood; now known as "Joseph of Arimathea," an honourable counselor, and a member of the Sanhedrin, listening oft to such discourse, thought ever of the boy of Nazareth, who was somewhere lost among the passing years.

In Galilee there had arisen One whose teachings and whose miracles, had oft been heard of in Jerusalem; some said He was a Prophet; but from obscurity He came, and only walked and taught among the poor and lowly, and His followers and associates were of that class called publicans and sinners, such as never were permitted to enter inside the temple walls. He was a wanderer without a home; known only by the name of Jesus, which of His birth

and place told naught, for many were named
Jesus. And as "Jesus" He was known and
loved in places where his wondrous power was
seen and known. And over all that land He
passed in silence, now here, now there, as
lightning flashes gleam when comes the eve-
ning hour's portentous calm ; still on, and on,
as one who has an urgent message to impart,
and whose allotted time is very short, so that
he may not tarry.

Marvelous His presence and His power. Thril-
ling oft the multitude with words of wisdom
and of truth ; then weeping o'er Jerusalem as a
woman might have wept. Nature knew Him ;
the listening angry waters, grow calm at His
command, and the mighty waves uphold Him
when He walks upon the sea.

But the emblematic light of life, was the
lesson that He brought. He taught it in the
healing of the sick, by giving sight unto the
blind, and by the dead restored to life again ;
but most of all He claimed the power to give
eternal life.

Thus while the life of Judah was ebbing fast
away and their last breath spent in unfruitful
argument, and sealed their eyes in darkness,
the God of Light and immortality walked to
and fro among them. Boldly He declared : " If
a man keep My saying he shall never see
death." " I only Am the Way, the Truth, the

Life." "I Am come, the King of light divine, to lighten this dark world, and lead the way to immortality beyond the skies." "I Am the resurrection, and the life."

"What marvel that the doctors of the law were full of wonder, and of doubt? That the wise Sanhedrin was dismayed, dreading such power as this? Yet unbelieving, with fine irony they argued: Surely the Lion of the tribe of Judah, would scorn to live with fishermen, and eat with publicans and sinners."

"It would be a noble sight when the children of Abraham should see the 'Star of Jacob' wander unattended along the dusty highways, so poor he had not where to lay His head." And only Joseph, ever remembering the boy of Nazareth, so like this Jesus and His life divine, thus pleading warns them: "Behold the whole world has gone out after Him, for never yet has man spake like this man, and though I know Him not, if He be of my brethren or no, gladly will I greet Him."

Then spake Caiaphas, bitterly: "This people who knoweth not the law, are all accursed; but thou, Joseph, whom I have known from youth, and who in the law wast strictly taught, what shall I say of thee?"

"Say what thou wilt, but unto thee say I, know that I am here to stand as one between the Gallilean and this mob; yea, and between Him and thee, so long as I do know that He has done no wrong, even though thou wast the High Priest of Jehovah." The face of Caiaphas then grew stern and dark; but one named Nicodemus, interposed: "Doth our law judge any man before it hear him and know what he doeth?" Then again arose a tumult, and they mocking said: "Art thou also of Galilee?" "Search and look, for out of Galilee ariseth no prophet." "And every man went unto his own house."

*   *   *   *   *

In the village of Bethany, at the foot of the Mount of Olives, within the shadow of the Holy City, Lazarus lay dying.

Where was the Master? Surely it is time the message found Him. "He whom thou lovest is sick." Afar the Shiloh heard, and the voice of love and faith that called Him from afar, was as music in His heart; and yet He lingered:

Four days had Lazarus been dead. Many who had loved him came to weep with Mary and with Martha; Joseph was there, and "Jesus of Nazareth" was coming--even now He trod the foot-hill path of Olivet, and as He walked He talked with His disciples. "Lazarus sleeps; it is the last time save one, I shall declare to them the power that Judah's Lion may divinely claim." Lazarus dead shall from the grave come forth and live again, to leave to ag es ye to come the truth of immortality.

"Standing by the grave of Lazarus, Jesus wept. Was it for Lazarus dead? Nay, but for those who in all time to come would for brief-space, rest them in the darkness; and for those whose hearts with anguish torn over scenes like this, that they might learn the message which from the grave of Lazarus has winged its way to all mankind, and filled the centuries of time with hope and light, and ever listening hear the echo of that mighty call to immortality: "*Come forth.*" "I am the resurrection and the life."

* * * * * *

Look! Joseph; Lazarus arisen from the dead, is naught of wonderment to thee, since thou hast seen the Gallilean Prophet, and hast heard him speak. It is the Boy of Nazareth, to manhood grown, Son of the carpenter, aye, and the "*Son of God.*" Swift hasten to Jerusalem, and warn the council ere it is too late.

Tell to them that Lazarus lives again, the lesson of the Acacia and the cedar is an eternal truth. Plead for the life of Judah's King, for thou hast seen His royal power, though masked in poverty; and His divinity is hidden in a human form so that they knew Him not. Oh! plead for Him with all thine eloquence, remembering the truths divine He taught thee in thy youth under the green of the cedar. Plead for

Him with all thine heart, for His dreams and visions of the great white city of God, grow plain unto you now, and you understand why in mortal hands the jewels from that city turned to dust.

Oh! plead for Him with all thy soul, remembering that shadow of the Cross, that darkened all His life; even now, glance up to Calvary, and from its summit see its shadow falling over Him. Yet all thy pleading is in vain: "His blood be upon us, and upon our children," and all the eloquence of earth were vain to hush the cry of "Crucify Him, Crucify."

All that is left for thee, is that thou mayest lay Him to repose in thine own tomb.

From the Mount the shadow falls; it lifts its mighty pall to Heaven; it darkens all the world; It covers all Jerusalem with sombre shade it never knew before: Joseph, watching and waiting, in agony second only to that of the Christ upon the Cross hears Him cry, as His sad eyes are upward turned to Heaven in appeal: "Eloi, Eloi, Lama Sabbacthani," and hiding his face, Joseph weeps as once before he wept, remembering His farewell:

"Eloi grant thee Peace; and if I
    sometime find, that City of the Night;
Joseph Akiba, you shall share with Me
    its light."

The Red Rose.

When this earth and time was new,
None other kind than white flowers grew ;
  The varied shades they since have shown,
  Were by a later cause made known.
    When angels visited the earth
  They brought the seeds that gave them birth :
Where 'er they found a barren spot
  They left the sweet " forget-me-not,"
And where they trod, the pansies eyes,
Serenely look up to the skies.
    The violet sheds its sweet perfume
  Where gaudy flowers refuse to bloom.
    The tiger-lilly's spotted clothes
  Grow where shade and damp repose ;
    Where solitude its sweetness gives,
  The arbutus and wild flower lives.
    And from the rocky mountain's crown
  The eidelweiss looks shyly down ;
  But as I said, when time was new,
  None other than the white flowers grew.
    The colour that we know as red,

Came as a symbol from the dead.
As Abel lay where he was slain,
The red blood gushed and left a stain :
 Close to where grew the snowy rose
 His body fell to death's repose.
  When the blood of life is shed
  All nature is disquieted,
  And when of passion crime was born,
  Nature was the first to mourn.
The stars looked out and sadly gazed,
Hoping the wrong would be erased.
Because they could not close their eyes,
They're ever twinkling in the skies ;
And since that time when earth was young,
The stars of heaven have never sung.
The moon rose with her silvery light,
Its searching gaze revealed the sight,
And rushing through the ether blue,
She hastened swiftly out of view,
Beseeching clouds to hide her face,
As she passed o'er the dreaded place.
 The air which yet no motion knew
Was thrilled with anguish through and through :
 It heard the spirit of the dead
Pass through it to the sky o'erhead :
 Along the path that it had flown
It left the echo of its moan
  The giant wind unfolds its wings,
And trembling with the murmurings ;
  Thus from its lethargy awoke

And the eternal calm was broke.
It starts away with frenzied force
Upon its wild resistless course ;
It sweeps the land with mighty breath
To rid it of the phantom death.
It told the story of the wrong,
In whispers as it rushed along,
When naught could for the sin atone,
Then did the wind in anguish moan.
And since that time, where'er it goes,
The wind has never known repose.
O'er all the earth it hides away
Never to rest, never to stay.
Sometimes in the twilight's glow
It whispers to us soft and low :
Anon it shakes the casement bar,
And calls, " I come to you from far,
Oh ! hear the message that I bear,
I am a spirit of the air."
Many the doors where it has knocked,
But few of them have been unlocked :
None courage have to bid it stay,
And sobbing low, it creeps away.
Since that time, when wrong is done,
The spirit of the murdered one
No human confidence may share,
But leaves its message in the air.
That night afar the wind had sped
And then by fascination led
When roseate blush the morning burned

Back to the scene again returned.
  The dead man lay as he had fell
But lo ! the night had woven a spell,
  The dew had fallen on his face,
And washed away the crimes dark trace,
  And over it thus wan and pale,
The spider threw a silvery veil.
  As if to hide the mark of sin
The earth had drank the red blood in ;
  It found the rosebush hidden heart
And there the story did impart,
  Up through its branch and tendrils crept
To the white roses, and they wept
  Tears which the blood transfusion fed.—
The roses turned from white to red.
  Thus Abel's blood "cried from the ground."
Without a voice without a sound.
  The wind passed o'er them shuddering :
The reddened leaflets to it cling,
  And drawn by its resistless force,
They follow with it in its course :
  And far away o'er land and tide,
It spread the petals far and wide.
  'Tis known to mortals since that time
Red, is the badge of every crime :
  Whatever form that shade may bring
It is the sign of suffering.
  Where discontent and passions rife,
There leads the blood-red flag of strife ;
  Its votaries have nursed the bud

That blossoms to the rose of blood.
  The history of every age,
Somewhere, sometime, on every page
  Is wrote with blood, with blood is red,
Of the living or the dead.
    When the world in darkness walked,
   Truth and innocence were mocked,
    And persecution led the way
Into the light of the " Red Ray."
   In its illuminating glow
The only light that age can show.
Upon that " Brotherhood " it fed,
  Whose mystic lucent light was spread
Where flames like these could never bind
  The mysteries therein enshrined.
  It drew into its warm embrace
    The tender light of woman's face
  They followed where the " Red Ray " led
   To garners of the martyred dead.
  If flames like those could purify,
    White were the souls it sent on high.

     *   *   *   *   *

The gift of perfect sacrifice
Was heaven-sent, without a price :
And thus the sins of all who erred,
Were to the Cross of Christ transferred ;
  The Christian's symbol it became,
An Oratorio of flame.
  Where shown the Cross there was a power
That ruled above the passing hour.

To Constantine the mystic sign
   Came as a symphony divine ;
Prelude to esoteric glow
   In future years it should bestow.
The glory of the Cross and Crown
In Omnipotence shining down,
Earth has no power to alienate
Nor time nor change, its force abate.
   It is the only horoscope
   That holds a sign of future hope ;
      And, with a faith grown infinite,
   The Templar follows in its light :
      Some mysteries to him revealed
   That are perhaps to others sealed.
But those who knew not of their laws,
And died not in the Templar's cause—
   —Whose faith was held inviolate
   However cruel was their fate,
      Whose life was given without a tear
   Or cry for mercy earth could hear
Dragged over sharp and cutting stones—
—None but the Master heard their moans
Torn to pieces, limb from limb,
Dying thus for love of him :
*Mother Earth, who gave them breath,

- - -

*Note. Quinta, a woman of Alexandria, was dragged
over sharp flint stones until torn and bleeding, and was
then stoned to death.
   Cecelia, a Roman matron, for refusing to renounce Chris-
tianity was thrown nude into a scalding bath, and was
afterward beheaded.

Was forced to smother them to death.*
Buried alive! Oh! God of Light,
  Never again send such a night.
    Oh! what of these who mild and meek,
Women whom the world calls weak,—
    —Women, who with mortal sight,
Never saw "Masonic Light;"
    No square nor compasse's design,
Modeled for them a life divine:
    Born in its truth and purity
They needed not its mystery,
    And lessons which the craftsman wrought
To them the Master's love had taught.
    Souls like these, when bodies die,
Pass on to light beyond the sky.
Happy for us who live today,
That darkened age has passed away,
  Drunken with fanatic zeal
How those centuries did reel.
    Creeds the light and forms the guide,
And back of them did evil hide.
    Now, from an atmosphere of doubt,
      The truth of God is shining out.
    Forms and creeds are thrust aside—
      --At least they are not deified.
    The worship of the heart and mind
      In spirit and in truth combined

---

*Note.--Three sisters, Agapa, Chione, and Irene, during
the persecution of the Christians, under Dioclesian, sub-
mitted to be buried alive, rather than sacrifice to idols.

The only worship He designed.
  And all religions interwove,
Rest only on the law of love.
  Nor form nor faiths this truth deny—
—As a man lives, so shall he die.

   *   *   *

  They always live and may be found
Who with roses red are crowned.
  Compassion have, where they are worn,
Know that a heart has cause to mourn.
  If to us upon the wing
Birds of Paradise shall sing,
  Some of that happiness transmit
To homes wherein the ravens sit.
  In halls of wealth as in a cot,
May live the " Lady of Shalott,"
  Whose woven pictures of the world
Their web-like tracery unfurled,
  The future and the past have crossed,
And in that heart all hope is lost.
  As silent waters first congeal,
They suffer most who least reveal,
  And only tender sympathies
Can reach to hidden hearts like these.
  Actions have a power of speech
No language ever yet could teach.
  And that is why never a word
To Heaven's record is transferred ;

Actions only are written there,
They are our hope or our despair.

* * * * *

Have you read that beautiful story ?
A legend of long ago,
Manifold are the beauties,
Its lesson may bestow.

'Tis that on Calvary's summit
Over that Cross renowned
When died the King who was crucified
That birds were fluttering round ;
No call, no sound did they utter,
But ever on restless wing,
As though 'twas a sorrow they could bor-
   row
Or help from afar could bring.

Perhaps they believed that Death was
  grieved,
And there with His mission at strife,
While the Nazarene waits, He hesitates
To strike at the God of Life ;
So He caused that pall of darkness to fall ;
When Christ in agony prayed,
To hide the sight from the Father of light,
For death itself was afraid.

Perhaps t'was the sight of the crimson
  light,
The dew by anguish distilled,
That the birds of the air knew the sign of

despair,
When the blood of Christ was spilled :
   For tis' said these birds, when he uttered
      the words,
" Lama Sabbacthini,"
   Caught hold of the nails where the flesh
      impales,
And with all their strength did try,
   To draw them away from the body of clay
—For the Prince of Peace was dead,—
They failed, we know, but wherever they go,
   They carry the badge of red.
Where their bosom was stained, the symbol
     retained,
   From the Master's blood in its flow,
By the robin's breast is their deed confessed,
   That all the world may know.

     *   *   *   *

Thus has the " Red Ray " found its way,
   Since first the world was new ;
Its lessons taught as time has wrought,
   While passing in review.
Symbol of strife, emblem of life,
   Dual in its power ;
Its beauties abide with the purified,
   When fades the passion flower.
Its roseate glow is burning low :
   Perhaps eternal light,
When earth is done and Heaven is won,
   Will turn the roses white.